A DIFFERENT TUNE

STORY
BRUCE WITTY

ILLUSTRATIONS
RICHARD LAURENT

COLORING
GAIL L. SUESS

Once upon a time,
in a land far away,
everyone looked alike
and did things the same way.

And everyone had
the same thing to say.
"Hello. What's new?
I'm fine. How are you?"

Each and every one
played a tune on his nose.
They played the same tune
with their eight tiny toes.

Into this land,
where all looked the same,
there came a stranger.
Bill was his name.

Bill was different.
It was easy to see.
Everyone thought Bill
was the wrong way to be.

Bill's nose was short,
not long like the rest.
Next to the others,
Bill failed every test.

13

Bill had only six toes.
The others had eight.
The others were early.
Bill always was late.

Because he was different,
Bill sometimes felt bad.
Bill tried to be happy
but sometimes was sad.

To cheer himself up,
Bill started to play
a tune on his nose
in his own special way.

Bill used his fingers
instead of his toes.
Bill used his fingers
to tune up his nose.

Beautiful music
Bill started to play.
The music was as sweet
as a warm summer day.

The music made everyone
open their ears.
It was music that everyone
wanted to hear.

Yes, Bill was different
from all of the rest.
Yes, Bill was different,
and his music was best.

Bill could not do
what the others could.
So Bill did what he could
and made something good.

Now Bill and the others
each play beautiful music
in their own special way.